Mouse Count

Ellen Stoll Walsh

Harcourt Brace Jovanovich, Publishers

San Diego   New York   London

Library of Congress Cataloging-in-Publication Data

Walsh, Ellen Stoll.

Mouse count/Ellen Stoll Walsh.

p.   cm.

Summary: Ten mice outsmart a hungry snake.

ISBN 0-15-256023-8

[1. Mice—Fiction. 2. Snakes—Fiction. 3. Counting.] I. Title.

PZ7.W1675Mn   1991

[E]—dc20   90-35915

First edition

A B C D E

The illustrations in this book are cut-paper collage.
The text type was set in ITC Modern by the Photocomposition Center, Harcourt Brace Jovanovich, Inc., San Diego, California.
Printed and bound by Tien Wah Press, Singapore
Production supervision by Warren Wallerstein and Ginger Boyer
Designed by Nancy J. Ponichtera and Camilla Filancia

For my nine sisters and brothers:
Sally, Leila, Mary, Nancy, Jane, Betsy,
Joe, George, and John,

and especially for Sally, the eldest,
and her husband, Jay,
intrepid seekers after truth.

GATE GATE PARAGATE PARASAMGATE
BODHI SWAHA!

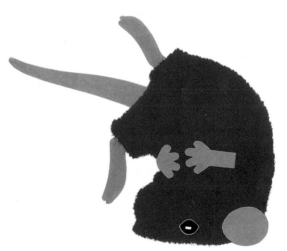

One fine day, some mice played in the meadow.
They were careful to watch for snakes.

But when the mice got sleepy, they forgot
about snakes . . .

and they all took naps.

While they slept, a hungry snake went looking
for dinner. On his way he found a nice big jar.

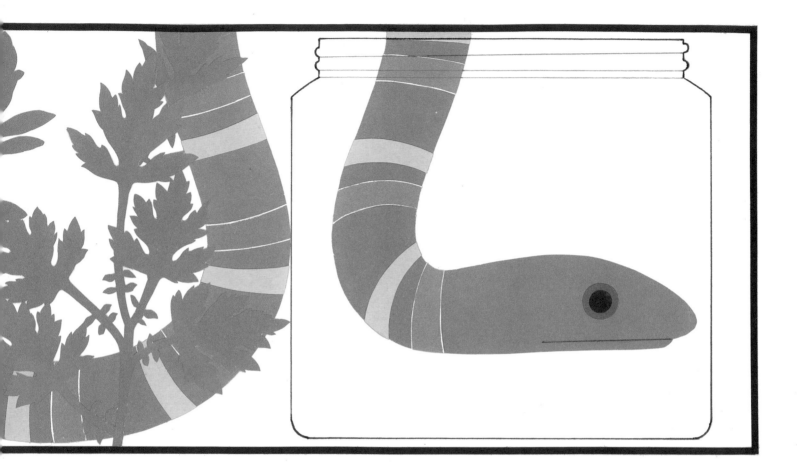

"I will fill this jar with dinner," he said.

It wasn't long before he found three mice—little, warm, and tasty, fast asleep.

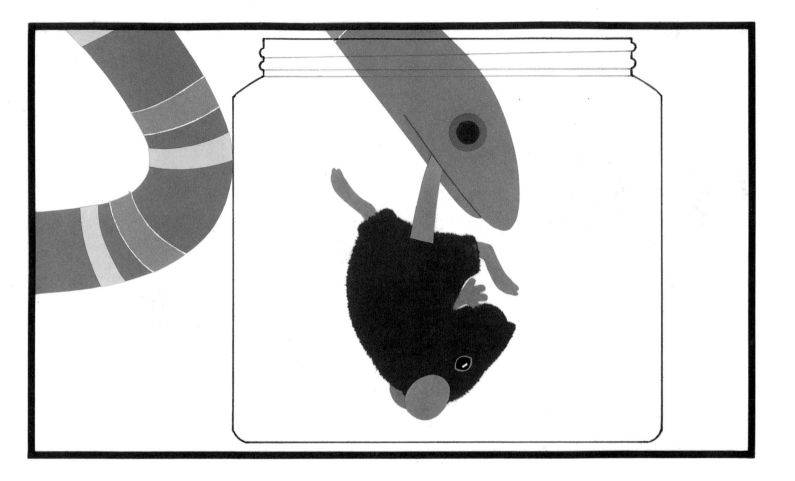

"First I will count them and then I will eat them up," said the snake. "Mouse Count! One . . .

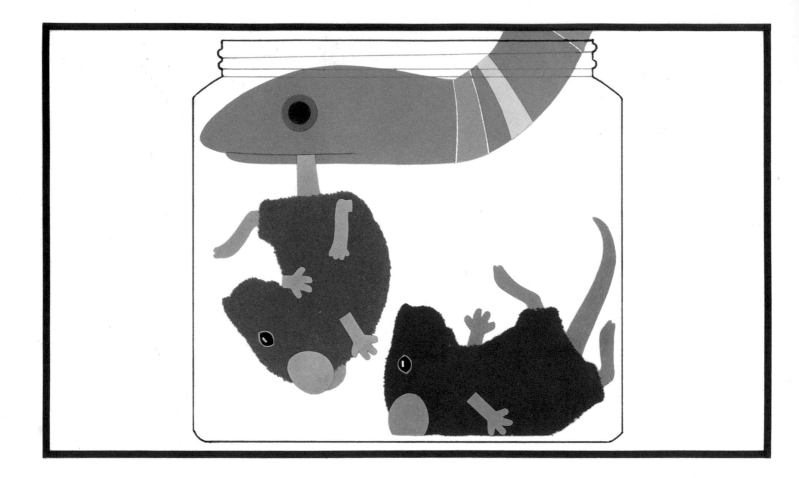

two . . .

three." He dropped them into the jar. But he was very hungry. Three mice were not enough.

Soon he found four more mice—little, warm,
and tasty, fast asleep.

And he counted them: "Four...

five . . .

six . . .

seven." But the snake was very, very hungry,
and seven mice were not enough.

At last he found three more mice—little, warm, and tasty, fast asleep. And he counted them:

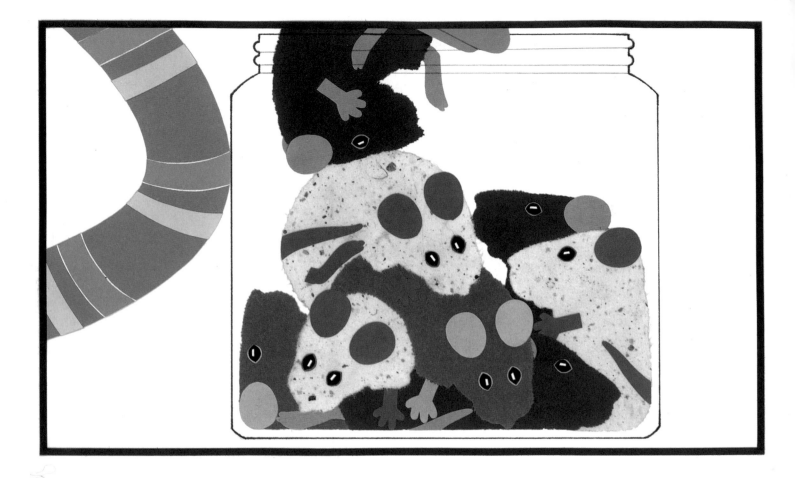

"Eight . . .

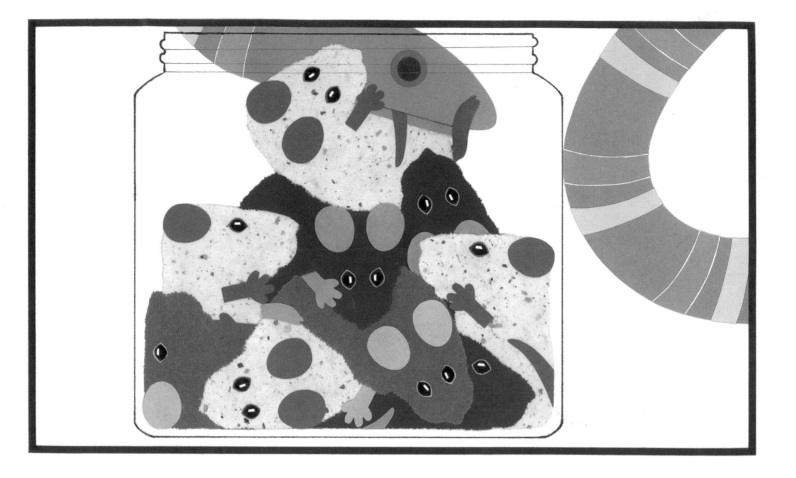

nine . . .

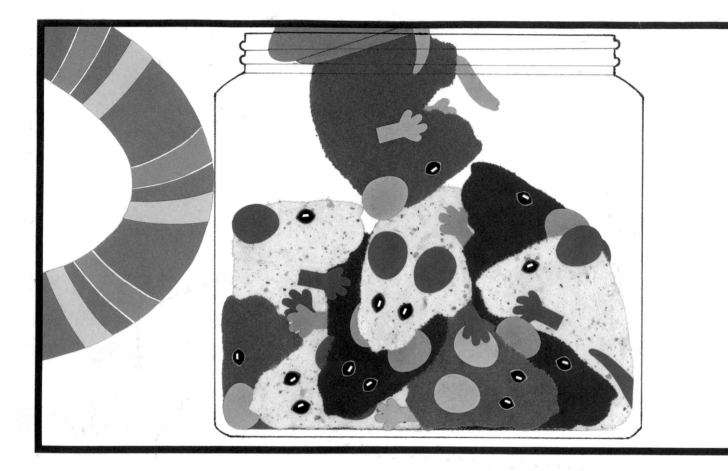

ten."

"Ten mice are enough. Now I am going to eat
you up, little, warm, and tasty," said the snake.

"Wait," said one of the mice. "The jar isn't full yet. And look at the big mouse over there."

The snake was very greedy. He hurried off to get
the big mouse.

And while he was gone, the mice rocked the jar
one way,

and another way,

until over it went.
"Ten, nine, eight, seven, six, five, four,

three, two, one." The little mice uncounted
themselves and ran home.

The snake reached the big mouse, but it was only
a cold, hard rock.

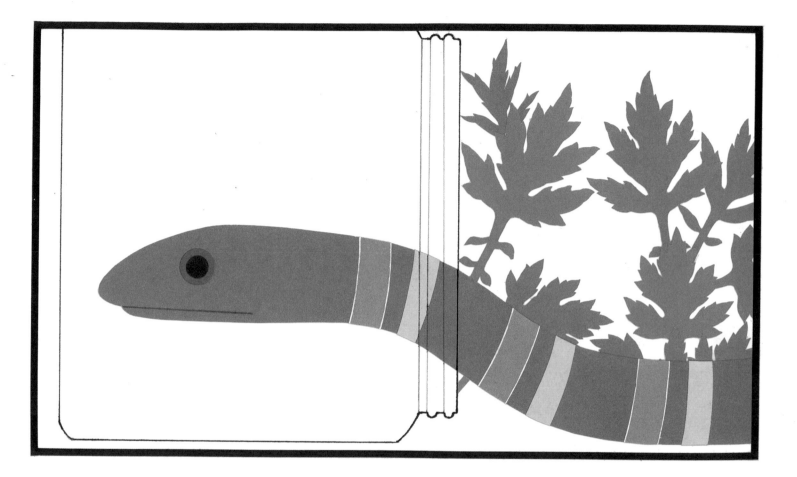

And when he got back, the jar was empty.

Precious in His Sight

PHOTOGRAPHY BY

DAVID DOBSON

WORD PUBLISHING
Dallas • London • Vancouver • Melbourne

*T*his book is dedicated to Olivia Vaccaro who is eight years old, to Chayne Vaccaro who is six years old, and to Elizabeth Vaccaro who is getting ready to be two years old. They are my closest and most precious friends in the younger generation.

You represent to me the future of missions. May Jesus use these pictures to sow in your hearts a seed of compassion for reaching your generation with his love.

When you look into the eyes of the less fortunate children in this book, please remember that Jesus loves them just as much as he loves you.

Thank you for your very special friendship and for all your prayers for me while I was traveling around the world capturing the images in this book. I love you.

Olivia

Chayne

Elizabeth

Foreword

When I look at the faces of the children in this book, I'm reminded of two special people in my life—Gavi and Ximena. They're the girls my family and I sponsor through Compassion International. We love these two girls as if they were our own, and we pray for them often as they pray for us.

I got involved with Compassion ten years ago for one extremely important reason—Compassion International is all about changing lives. Not only does this ministry help meet the physical, social, and economic needs of children, its first objective is to share the gospel with all of its kids. Because of that, Gavi and Ximena now know the Lord personally, and they have come to understand the power of prayer and the sweetness of fellowship through the letters we write to one another.

By purchasing this book, you, too, will share in this ministry that changes lives. A portion of the profits from this book will be donated to Compassion International. But why not take this one step further? There are children like Gavi and Ximena still waiting for sponsors. To find out more, check out the information at the end of the book.

By the way, thank you for buying this book and investing in the lives of children all over the world.

Michael W. Smith

Acknowledgments

My Parents, Dwight and Anita Dobson: Thank you for giving me the best childhood a photographer could ever have and for encouraging the gift of creativity in my life. Thank you for loving me and dedicating me to God, for continually supporting and encouraging me in everything He has allowed me to do. Thank you for letting me go and do what God has called me to do and for trusting Him to take care of your son. And thank you for teaching me to respect and admire the cultures we have lived in, to treat everyone as equal regardless of social or economic standing.

My Brothers, Paul and Andre: Thanks for being the most incredible brothers I could ever have. Thanks for laughing at all my jokes, for putting up with my weird ideas, for letting me experiment on you with my camera, for covering for me when I needed it most, and for knocking me back in line when things go crazy.

Uncle Wayne, Aunt Katherine, Alison, and Anita: Thank you for all your interest, support, encouragement, and advice from day one. Thank you for being the closet family while we lived overseas and for the support we needed when we moved back home. Thank you for being such a great example and for being such fun.

Grandma and Grandpa Dobson and Francis: Thank you for your strong foundation and relationship with the Lord. I am truly blessed because of your unceasing prayers and encouragement. Thank you for praying me through every situation, circumstance, and adventure in my life. I would never be who I am or where I am without you. I love you.

The Vaccaro Family: Thank you for letting me be a part of your beautiful family. Thank you for being my older brother and sister, and for the privilege of being your daughter's godfather—what an honor that is for me. Thank you for all the guidance, advice, interest, and support you have been in my life and career.

Ron Barefield: Thank you for believing that I was the man for the job and for taking a chance on a young missionary kid with a camera. Thanks for sending me to the most remote parts of the mission world in the hottest, most miserable times of the year or to Siberia in the "cool" season. Thanks for accepting those collect calls, for being on my side when I needed it most, and for believing in me and what God is doing in my life.

David Burdine and Don Beard: Thank you for helping a young missionary kid with a huge goal in life and a desire to use his talents in photography to help others around the world. Thank you for your interest, support, advice, and guidance over the years. Thank you for letting me be a part of what you are doing in missions.

Terri Gibbs: Thank you for tracking me down and getting me and my pictures to Word, Inc. Thank you for all your help in making this dream come true. I appreciate everything you have done for me.

Jack Countryman: Thank you for believing in my work and for offering me the opportunity to work with you on this project. May God use this book to help thousands of needy children around the world to have a better life.

Tim and Avonna Schirman: Thank you for being my friends and for all the many things you have taught me over the years. Thanks for always fixing my problems and for dealing with my technical impatience! Thank you for knowing more about every piece of equipment I own than I do and for sharing your theories of being a cameraman. I am especially grateful for the countless hours you have invested in my footage to share the story of what God is doing through missionaries. May God greatly bless you for your commitment to Him through excellence and creativity.

Tim Keating: Thank you for taking a special interest in me as your photo student and for developing the talents that God has given me. Thank you for being a crucial part of His plan for my life and for being a friend and a mentor. I wish that you could be here now to see the results of your patient investment in my life.

Robb Arron Gordon: Thank you for your encouraging and supportive friendship through the years, your incredible style (FDM), appreciation of art, sense of humor, and attention to detail. Thanks for all your help in capturing so many of the images in this book.

Kim Smith: Thank you for being the most beautiful girl in the world in seventh and eighth grades—you were my inspiration to pick up the camera and start all of this. Thank you for being a big part of God's plan for my life.

*G*rowing up as a missionary kid in Calcutta, India, and Cairo, Egypt, I was exposed to two of the most intense cultures in the world. What fascinating places to grow up as a young boy. There were always markets, temples, and back alleys to wander through and explore. These colorful experiences made a strong impact on my young mind. I will never forget the streams of humanity I pushed through on my daily quest to see what surprises lay round the next corner. I always wanted to be an explorer.

I found I could record my adventures by borrowing my father's camera. Now I had a way to capture the eyes and catch a glimpse of the souls of the fascinating and beautiful people around me. My favorite people to photograph are children and older people. Children—with their innocent mischievousness—and the wealth of experience I find in the wrinkles of the elderly, constantly compel me to take one more roll of film around one more corner.

When I was in high school I often wondered what I would do with my talent in photography for God's kingdom. One night I made a deal with God. I told Him that I would go anywhere at any time as long as He provided the way. Close to one hundred countries later, I have come to see what a privileged life God has blessed me with—a life rich with fond memories of adventure and seeing firsthand what God is doing around the world among the people He loves.

When I look through my camera into the eyes of the people of the world, I see a part of their souls. In most of their eyes I see a longing for truth, a desire to share that saving grace we sometimes take for granted. In the eyes of the children I see the future, a chance that perhaps we can reach this generation with the gift of eternal life.

I trust that as you look through this book and see the faces of children all over the world, God will give you a glimpse of their lives that will increase your love and concern for these little ones.

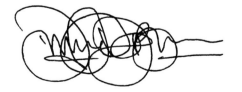

David Dobson
Santa Barbara, California
August 1997

O God, an older hand will lead the young. A hand they cling to trustfully and follow. But where? To what? May the children of the world be lead to you . . . to eternal life through your Son.

When a Buddhist Lama dies the monks search for a child in whom they believe the Lama's spirit has been reincarnated. They felt this little boy was the one chosen to be the next Lama. He holds the hand of his guardian who will oversee his training in a Buddhist monastery.

—*Katmandu, Nepal*

A little boy leans against the doorway in Zaire, East Africa.

ometimes, children are lost and afraid. They cannot find their way alone. Guide them, Father, lead them with your strong hand.

The baby girl stands wrapped in her mother's shawl.—Darjeeling, India.

*R*ock a bye baby,

Jesus is waiting,

to give you his love

and a home up above.

No need to fear

for Jesus is near.

Let his gentleness surround you

like mother's warm hug.

From Bhutan, the little girl dresses in traditional clothing.

*T*he hands that formed the universe molded and shaped each child. Each pair of eyes and button nose were sculptured with great care. Thank you, God, for giving life to every incredible kid!

*N*orth and south
and east and west
May the Savior's name
be blest;
Everywhere beneath the sun,
As in heaven, Thy will
be done.

Give me food that I
may live;
Every naughtiness forgive;
Keep all evil things away
From Thy little child
this day.

W. CANTON
1845-1926

A boy in Brazil laughs in the window of a house built up on wooden stilts.

*In Calcutta a little girl washes the family pots and pans. She takes
care of her brothers and sisters while her parents work.*

O God, in a city of nearly thirteen million people, you see each busy child. You hold each hopeful dream like a star in the sky. You've counted the hairs on every little head. You've formed each wonderful boy and girl exactly like you said—to remind us of your love.

A young boy stands in the doorway of a Buddhist temple in Bhutan.

e who can
reach a child's heart can
reach the world's heart.

RUDYARD
KIPLING

*B*less the dainty
girls who build castles of
fancy on painted chairs . . .

Sitting on the verandah outside their father's office,
two girls from Ivory Coast enjoy a piece of candy.

Bless the carefree boys

who splash and laugh at

the water well...

Bless the child who plays

with beetles and marbles

and jump ropes... please,

Father, just bless them all!

What fun to play in a water fountain in Morocco. In this town there is no indoor plumbing in individual homes, so everyone comes to the fountain for water.

Full of happy energy, this little boy passes time in the hot Jamaican summer playing with his friends.

This little light
of mine,

I'm gonna let it shine.

Oh, this little light
of mine,

I'm gonna let it shine.

This little light of mine,

I'm gonna let it shine.

Let it shine,

Let it shine,

Let it shine.

TRADITIONAL
SPIRITUAL

Children who suffer from malnutrition relish a balanced meal at a missionary station in Benin.

A young girl from the Aka tribe of Northern Thailand wears a traditional tribal costume.
The Aka people are a proud and noble people with an ancient heritage.

f all God's natural wonders, can anything match the beauty of a child? We can't help but see your handiwork, Father, in the sparkle of shining eyes, the brightness of a smile. All the crayons in the world couldn't paint a prettier picture, just waiting to know your love.

A Child's Prayer

*M*ake me,

dear Lord, polite and kind

To every one, I pray.

And may I ask you how

you find

Yourself, dear Lord, today?

JOHN

BANNISTER

TABB

A young girl in Siberia smiles shyly for the camera.

*"*efore I formed
you in the womb I knew
you..."*

JEREMIAH 1:5

*While her parents stand in line at a free medical clinic in Calcutta, India, the baby girl plays
in the dirt. Her parents believe the necklace and bracelet will ward off evil spirits.*

Father, when I look into her shining eyes I wonder what the future will bring. Will her designs be worn by all? Her music thrill millions? Will her hands create exquisite art? What fun to dream of tomorrow's possibilities— especially when they are divinely blessed.

In Beijing, China, a family visits the ancient Emperor's vacation home.
The children play hide-and-seek among the ancient stone columns.

This little girl belongs to the Land Divers, the original tribe of Pentecost Island, Vanuatu. A bush tribe, the Land Divers live off of wild animals from the jungle and fresh produce they grow in small garden plots.

*L*et the Savior's

gentle call

Reach the heart of one

and all,

That the whole round world

may own

Christ is King, and Christ

alone.

ANONYMOUS

*L*ittle hands to play in the mud. Little eyes to see where to go. Little ears to hear about Jesus. Father, may it be so.

In India a girl plays in the sewer mud with her friends.
She wears a good-luck charm around her neck.

What hope does a young girl have without your gift of love and eternal life, Father? You alone can forge faith in her heart, faith to light her path when darkness falls across it, faith to believe in your Son.

To help her family, this girl in India sells goods at the market. The red dot on her forehead indicates that she has said her prayers for the day in the Hindu temple.

Father, they are so old, these little ones who grow up too soon to play. When their lives are a constant struggle ... when the weariness of the world weighs them down ... lift them with your love.

Hands and face stained from his work, a little boy in Egypt gathers coal to sell for his parents.

This young girl works all day to collect firewood to sell or trade in the large open-air market in Goma, Zaire.

If you want your market produce delivered fresh to your door, this young man will fill your order at the market and bring it to your home. He works for a vegetable vendor in Rangoon, Burma.

Although just six years old, this tiny girl from Cambodia rides the ferry back and forth across the river all day to sell her bread to the passengers.

A young girl in Egypt comforts and cares for her baby brother during the day while her parents work.

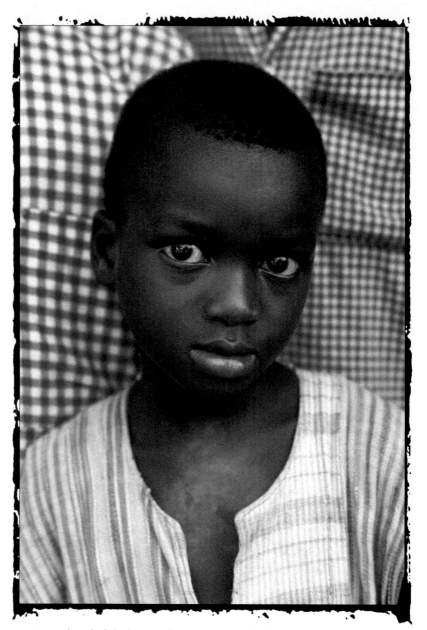

*W*hat can

I give Him,

Poor as I am?

If I were a shepherd

I would bring a lamb,

If I were a Wise Man

I would do my part,—

Yet what I can I give Him,

Give my Heart.

CHRISTINA
ROSSETTI

Because he is deaf, this boy attends a missionary school in Benin for the hearing impaired.
Without this special training he would have to beg in the streets in order to survive.

$\mathcal{B}$ut Jesus said,
"Let the little children
come to Me, and do not
forbid them; for of such is
the kingdom of heaven."

MATTHEW 19:14

A group of children in Malawi gather to have their picture taken. The older ones
take care of the younger ones while their parents work in the fields.

Thank you, God, for special friends. They share our days, they make life fun. They make us smile as bright as the sun. But only you can be the very best Friend of all—not only for the children but for grown-ups too.

Two smiling Indian girls dressed in traditional costumes participate in a wedding.

A beaming girl in Ivory Coast is glad to show off her sprightly hairdo for the camera.
Children in West Africa have a strong sense of personal style.

Love is little,
   love is low
Love will make my
   spirit grow;
Grow in peace, grow in light
Love will do the thing
   that's right.

ANONYMOUS

Spending long days all alone, a farmer boy in Malawi is responsible to care for the family cows. He makes sure they don't run away or get stolen.

peak gently to the

young, for they

Will have enough to bear;

Pass through this life as

best they may,

'Tis full of anxious care.

SHAKER PRAYER

With great skill and dexterity, a young boy throws out his fishing net in hopes of catching food for his family to eat and to sell. He fishes in the river that flows between Benin and Togo.

There is no running water in the homes of this village in Siberia. The son of one family pumps water from the old street pump.

A young child in Zaire helps his family to harvest their rice. If he is old enough to be away from his mother's watchful eye, he is old enough to work in the fields.

Tears roll down a little cheek during a tender moment in rural Egypt.

Growing up can be such fun, but not all the time. Some days bring joy and laughter—others bring heartache and tears. Look down on the children of the world, Father, to dry their tears and heal their hurts. Bring hope . . . bring happiness.

A smiling boy in Chile stops playing with his toy car just long enough to have his picture taken.

 h to be six years old again. With two empty pockets and a head full of schemes and a little red car that can drive to the moon. May the boyish heart belong to you Father, to walk on the path of your true Word.

One of the major crops of Sri Lanka is tea. Only women are used to harvest the fragile leaves. They begin training to pick the leaves when they are very small. The tea bushes are planted in dense rows about 12 inches apart. The tea pickers must always be watchful of poisonous snakes that hide deep in the leaves.

Once again, dear Lord,

    we pray

For the children far away,

Who have never even heard

Name of Jesus, sweetest word.

Teach them, O Thou heav'nly
        King,
All their gifts and praise
        to bring
To Thy Son, who died to prove
Thy forgiving, saving love.

M. J. WILCOX,
1888

*A girl from the Aka tribe of Thailand wears a traditional headdress of
silver and beads for a ceremonial celebration.*

Three boys play in the fields outside their village in Siberia.

*A*bove the place

where children play

A window opens, far away,

For God to hear the

happy noise

Made by His little girls

and boys.

CHARLES DALMON

*The carnival haunted house at a school in Guatemala
is just too scary for this little girl . . .*

. . . but she will smile if you take her picture.

Tears one minute, smiles the next. At age five, joy and sorrow are an instant mix. Let the children come to you Father, hide them in your arms. Double their smiles and dry their tears.

*A*lthough God
loves the whole wide
world
And blesses every part,
I think he has a special
place
For children in His heart.

I think He cherishes their
smiles,
Their eagerness and mirth,
And their appreciation of
The wonders of His earth...

All children in a special way
Belong to God above,
And I am sure He favors
them
With everlasting love.

JAMES J.
METCALFE

*A mother from a tribal mountain village in Guatemala holds her daughter. She weaves
the highly decorative costumes and blankets by hand to sell in the market.*

Children of Guatemala dress like angels and walk in a religious procession from their village to the church.
The villagers dye sawdust white and place it carefully on the ground to form the pathway.

Left without a family, this girl in Romania sleeps in a rusty train car at night and walks the streets by day to beg for money and food.

We pray for the children who sleep in rusty railway cars at night and walk the streets begging by day. It does not seem fair, Father. They should have mothers and fathers to tuck them in at night. They should not have to beg for food. Let us be willing to step out of our comfortable world, our downy feather beds—and DO something to help them.

*A deaf girl in Sri Lanka learns how to do fine needle work at a
vocational training school for the hearing impaired.*

ll things
bright and beautiful,
all creatures great and small,
All things wise and wonderful,
the Lord God made them all.

CECIL FRANCES
ALEXANDER
1848

A small girl in Katmandu stands between two lion-god statues at the entrance to a temple.
The red mark on her forehead shows that she has said her prayers for the day.

They hear slamming doors, hurried steps of fear, faces contorted in anger. There are many kinds of snapping demons in their lives.

...When they are
bewildered and confused,
may they find your
comfort and love, O God—
and please keep them safe.

*In spite of his family's poverty, a young man in Jamaica stands
gaily dressed near the doorway of his home.*

*Pausing at the temple wall, this young woman reflects on the
day's ceremonies at the altar in a temple in India.*

*S*imple pleasures for a cuddly treasure. Joy wrapped up in a baby boy. May the angels guard this treasure so he can grow to know God's love.

The son of a vegetable vendor, a baby boy plays with the tomatoes in his father's market stall in Chile.

Abandoned by his parents, a Romanian toddler enjoys a warm bowl of soup at one of the many government orphanages.

 child is left alone without a mother's love. Yet your love, O God, can bring another who will fill the hungry tummy and pour kindness into the lonely heart. A hug and a kiss would be nice too.

*A girl from the mountains of Darjeeling, India,
carries her dog, a Lhasa Apso.*

*A warm, furry puppy gets a tight hug on
a cold summer day in Siberia.*

*T*hank you, Father,
for pets. For the snugly love
of a puppy...

the fuzzy fur of a monkey,
the glowing green eyes
of a cat, ... even a scary,
squirmy snake. Bless the
children, playing with
their pets—and bless
the little pets.

*In Sri Lanka the children play
with pet monkeys.*

A young Buddhist monk in Bhutan plays with his cat.

*When you live in the Amazon jungles a boa
constrictor makes an interesting pet.*

At an orphanage in North Viet Nam, an elderly man teaches a young girl how to read English. A French lesson is written on the black board.

*P*raise the Lord from

the earth,...

Both young men and

maidens;

Old men and children.

PSALM 148:7, 12

In Beijing, China, the government allows families to have only one child. This boy's father, who is a soldier, dresses his son in a miniature military uniform in hopes that he will one day be a soldier too.

*L*ook down upon the future leaders of our world, Father. Grant your wisdom to the young ones who will one day walk at the front of the line. May the violent passions and hatreds of their fathers' generation be forgiven and forgotten in theirs.

This boy in Calcutta, India works as a mechanic's apprentice.
One day he will be a mechanic himself.

Three young Buddhist monks wait for the bus that
will take them to the temple school in Sri Lanka.

Prayer for Children

We pray for children

who put chocolate fingers
everywhere,
who like to be tickled...

And we pray for those...
who never "counted
potatoes,"
who are born in places we
wouldn't be caught dead...

We pray for children
who bring us sticky kisses
and fistfuls of dandelions
who sleep with the dog and
bury goldfish...

And we pray for those . . .

who have no safe blanket

to drag behind,

who can't find any bread to

steal . . .

For those we smother,

and for those who will grab

the hand of anybody

kind enough to offer.

INA HUGHS

*A frightened child clings to her mother's grass skirt
on the South Pacific island of Vanuatu.*

*Because this boy belongs to the Sikh religious group of New
Delhi, India, he cannot cut his hair. He learns from his
father how to tie it in a knot under his scarf.*

Fascinated by the activities of the market below, this little Nepali boy watches from the security of his balcony. The hanging flowers are religious symbols.

Gentle Jesus,
King of kings,
Yet the Lord of little things,
Though but small and
young I be,
From Thy glory smile
on me.

RODNEY
BENNETT

By cleaning the dirt and debris from a basket of peanuts, a small child in Zaire helps her mother prepare curry for supper.

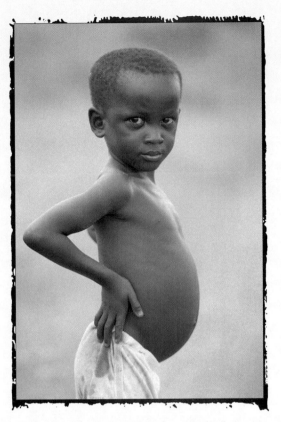

Like many other children in West Africa, this little boy's big tummy is a sign that he doesn't get the proper nourishment for his body.

*F*ather, our hearts ache for desperate children who must rummage through refuse for food. From east to west they forage in filth and still go hungry.

In Brazil a boy rummages through a vast garbage dump to find things to sell. If he is lucky he might also find something to eat.

...May we reach out to help them generously with gratitude for our abundance—and forgive us for grumbling about soggy fries.

Three boys in the Philippines rest beside their lean-to. They live and work in the garbage dump where they search for useful debris that someone will buy or exchange for food.

*R*emember now thy Creator in the days of thy youth, while the evil days come not, nor the years draw nigh, when thou shalt say, I have no pleasure in them.

ECCLESIASTES
12:1

Leaning out the window of the family car, a young girl in Cuba waits for her mother to return from shopping. New cars have not been sold in Cuba since the 1950s.

Thousands of children around the world live on the streets and survive by their own wits. In Chile, a street boy sits in a doorway near the fruit market to eat a melon he "rescued" from a pile of trash.

God bless smudged faces, scabby elbows, and muddy feet. Bless dirty boys, Lord, especially those who have no mother to wash their hands or clean their clothes.

*J*esus loves the little children,

From his home in a remote part of India, this boy walks three days to attend boarding school. At noon the students all take their mattresses outside to air out.

...all the children of

the world.

A bright, red hat provides warmth for a young girl as she works on a tea plantation in Sri Lanka. She clears brush and debris from between the rows of tea plants.

Wearing the traditional farming clothes of Egypt, a boy rides his donkey to town.

He prayeth well,
who loveth well.
Both man and bird and
beast.
He prayeth best, who
loveth best.
All things both great and
small;
For the dear God who
loveth us,
He made and loveth all.

SAMUEL TAYLOR
COLERIDGE

This boy's family are sheep herders who live high in the Andes Mountains near Cuzco, Peru. He plays his flute while tending the sheep. His family sells some of the wool and uses some to weave into fabric for their own clothing.

Father, thank you for children whose lives don't revolve around video games, Golden Books, and films. Let us see the world through their eyes; let our hearts hear their song.

*C*hild's eyes to see,
child's ears to hear—
God grant to me
That vision clear.

J. M. WESTRUP

*A carefree boy sits on the back of an ancient demon god in
Viet Nam. The statue frowns, but the boy smiles.*

Father, you are not afraid of our questions. You understand when we wonder why. The world is full of little ones whose best efforts can't figure life out. Hear their puzzled perplexities and may they know you, Father, the answer to all of life.

Brightly dressed in blue, an Indian girl helps her father buy food from the outdoor market for their supper.

So many children tremble in superstition and fear. Father, only you can clear their sight and give them peace.

When he was crippled by polio in infancy, this young boy's parents placed him in a Hindu temple to be raised as a Sadu. The white powder on his body is a sign that he belongs to the temple. He wears prayer beads around his neck.

An Indian mother paints black around her baby's eyes believing it will protect her daughter from evil spirits.

*Dressed in religious finery and prayer beads, a little child
from Goa, India, participates in spiritist worship.
Religious markings decorate her face.*

A young Buddhist monk lights prayer candles in a temple in Tibet.

...Wherever children
crouch in fear and tremble
in the night let sparkles of
your truth bring them light
and freedom from despair.

*T*hou who once on

mother's knee

Wast a little child like me,

When I wake or go to bed,

Lay Thy hands upon my

head;

Let me feel Thee very near,

Jesus Christ, my Savior

dear....

F.T. PALGRAVE,
1824 - 1897

In Saigon, a baby rides on a little bike-seat in front of his mother and his father. The family rides together on one bike.

*F*ather, so many children have been cheated by the evil in the world. We don't understand why they must suffer because of the greed, pride, and ignorance of others. Be merciful to these who have the right to cry, yet choose to smile instead.

Because his mother was exposed to Agent Orange during the Viet Nam war, this boy was born without arms or legs. He sits on the sidewalk in Cambodia with an aluminum pot to beg for money. His mother sits in the park nearby to watch after him and help him. His name in English means "Lucky."

You notice the diligent children, Father, willing and eager to please. What precious packages of potential just waiting to be grown up. Help them, Father, when their arms grow weary and their strength is gone.

In Egypt a girl carries a heavy load of dead wood and sticks to help her father clear a field.

...Ease the load a little,
whether wooden sticks...
or stubborn sheep—and
let each child know that
you care.

A shepherd boy in Romania takes care of the family sheep. His parents depend on him to lead the sheep to good pasture and to protect them from predators.

Let me learn of
Jesus;
He is kind to me.
Once He died to save me
Nailed upon the tree.

If I go to Jesus,
He will hear me pray,
Make me pure and holy,
Take my sins away....

FANNY J.
CROSBY,
1820 - 1915

A deaf girl in Sri Lanka holds her hands together and bows to say hello.
She lives in a vocational training center for the hearing impaired.

In the arms of God, the biggest troubles grow small. Thank you Father, for the quiet moments. In the stillness we remember your goodness.

A young Costa Rican student takes a moment from his studies to share a smile.

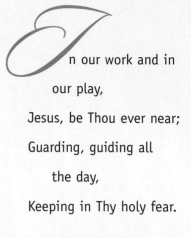

*I*n our work and in
our play,
Jesus, be Thou ever near;
Guarding, guiding all
the day,
Keeping in Thy holy fear.

W. C. DIX,
1837 - 1898

In this lagoon in West Africa the houses are built on stilts.
This girl rows her canoe from one end of the floating
village to the other on an errand for her mother.

A village girl in Africa takes a moment to rest in the shade.

Pita bread is a staple food in Egypt. This girl buys it fresh from the oven for her family.

ou sent bread from heaven for the Israelites, Father, and you nourish the grains of the earth so we can bake white bread, brown bread, sourdough bread...even pita bread. Thank you for all the delicious breads in the world, and thank you for being the Bread of Life to feed the hungry souls of the world.

A Little Child May Know

little child

may know

Our Father's name of Love.

'Tis written o'er the

earth below

And on the sky above.

A Jewish boy at the wailing wall in Jerusalem reads Scripture and prays. He is part of the Hasidim, a Jewish sect that is highly devoted to the strict observance of ritual law.

Around me when I look

His handiwork I see;

This world is like a

    picture book

To teach His love to me.

JANE E. LEESON,
1807 - 1882

*Outside Katmandu, Nepal, young boys who are training to be Buddhist
monks take time out from their religious duties to fly a kite.*

Water from the village well refreshes a boy on a hot summer day in Zaire.
Everyone in the village uses the water from one central well.

The water running at the village well might dry up tomorrow. The corn growing in the fields might turn brown and shrivel. But you, O God, will never cease to feed our hungry souls and give us help in time of need.

The tiniest of the Aka tribe people in Thailand, this baby wears a traditional embroidered hat. She rides in a shawl on her mother's back.

Sleep, baby, sleep!
Our Savior loves His sheep:
He is the Lamb of God
 on high,
Who for our sakes came
 down to die.
Sleep, baby, sleep!

ANONYMOUS

A boy enjoys soup for lunch in Bangkok, Thailand.

A bowl of steaming egg-drop soup. A coconut or a yam. A bright yellow banana or a fish caught on the run...

We thank you, Father, for the food you provide for all the hungry little tummies around the world, and we ask that hungry little souls will also be fed from your living Word.

Caught in the middle of a tropical monsoon storm, a child from a village in India pauses in the rain just long enough to show off her fish.

*When the children of Bali, Indonesia, pray in the temple, the
priest presses sticky rice on their foreheads to bless them.*

In this big wide
world of ours,
God has made enough
sunshine
For everyone to have
a share,
Sometime . . . Somewhere.

ZELDA DAVIS
HOWARD

*Children who attend preschool in Brazil learn how to read
and how to write in cursive from age three.*

Jesus, Friend of
little children,
Be a Friend to me;
Take my hand, and ever
keep me
Close to thee.

Teach me how to grow in
goodness,
Daily as I grow;
Thou hast been a child,
and surely
Thou doest know....

WALTER J.
MATHAMS,
1851 - 1931

This boy lives in a fishing village in Bali, Indonesia. His parents made the small catamaran so he can be prepared to fish from large catamarans when he is older.

On the Marshall Islands, a boy and his dog enjoy an afternoon of leisure in a canoe. Perhaps they are pretending to be pirates.

Blessings on thee,
little man,
Barefoot boy, with cheek of tan!...
With the sunshine on thy face,
Through thy torn brim's jaunty grace;

From my heart I give thee joy,—
I was once a barefoot boy!

JOHN GREENLEAF
WHITTIER

*F*ather, when the storms of life rage against this young boy, let his roots be planted in you, strong to weather the gale. And while he may not see much more for himself than what is right in front of him, guide him and use him to accomplish great things.

A proud Egyptian boy poses in front of the great pyramids of Giza, a symbol of his country's vast historical heritage.

The little ones follow in the footsteps of their fathers. They walk the ancient paths. Show them the path that leads to you, Father, to eternal life and joy.

Two brothers in Bali, Indonesia, are dressed in their Sunday best to worship in the Hindu temple. They wear traditional clothing inspired from the Indian influence that came to Bali through trade.

Four Muslim boys study from Islamic text books in a mosque in Singapore. They wear these hats only for religious studies.

...May their feet find
that path and their hearts
accept your truth.

School children in West Africa try to climb out the window of the school house to have their picture taken.

Hosanna,

    be the children's song

To Christ, the children's King.

His praise to whom their souls

    belong,

Let all the children sing.

Hosanna, then, our song

    shall be,

Hosanna to our King.

This is the children's jubilee,

Let all the children sing.

JAMES
MONTGOMERY,
1771 - 1854

*F*ather, surely your heart breaks like ours to think that innocent orphans sit alone and wonder why—no one bothers to love them. Send someone to tell them of your love, to pray for them, to take them home.

Since the fall of Communism in Romania many families can no longer support their large families. Hundreds of children are abandoned by their parents and sent to orphanages to become wards of the state.

*O*ne week they are

boys, and then

Next week they are slim

young men

Standing very still and lean,

perilously scrubbed and

clean.

Enjoy each small boy while

you can,

Tomorrow there will be a

man....

ROBERT P.
TRISTRAM COFFIN

*A young cowboy in Chile, just age five, wants to be
a rancher like his father when he grows up.*

*A father and his two sons from the mountain village of
Titichango in Guatemala, bring produce from
their ranch to sell in the city market.*

A group of children who live along the Amazon river, study their school books at night by the light of a kerosene lamp.

Soft falls the night,
The day grows dim,
To Thee I lift my evening
hymn,
O Lord of dark and light.

My hands I raise,
A little spire,
And send my voice up high
and higher
To thee in happy praise....

EDITH KING

A Child's Morning Prayer

Look down on me,
   a little one,
Whose life on earth is
      but begun:
Dear Savior, smile on me.

Watch over me from day
      to day,
And when I work, or when
      I play,
Dear Savior, smile on me.

Help me to do Thy holy will,
With lovely thoughts my
      mind to fill:
Dear Savior, smile on me.

J .   K I R B Y

Although she is only 5 years old, this little girl in Cambodia runs in and out among the cars leaving the ferry boat trying to sell some bananas. She must be careful of being crushed by the mad dash of cars in a hurry to get off the boat.

You take care of sparrows, Father, and you take care of kids. When they must beg by day only to fall asleep hungry at night, help them to find you, to move out of the darkness into your light.

Street kids in India walk through the market begging for food.

A boy from Nepal proudly wears a homespun beanie cap. The red dots on his forehead signify that he has been to the Hindu temple to say his prayers.

A boy says his prayers to a stone-faced god...earnest prayers of no avail. Give us your compassion, Father, for the countless children who need to know there is a living God. One whose Son hugged the boys and girls and brought them a gift—eternal life.

An Opportunity to Help

Every day 34,000 children die of starvation and preventable diseases. The organization listed below is dedicated to providing for the physical and spiritual development of children around the world. If you would like to reach out in love to impoverished children there will never be a better time than today.

Compassion International

P.O. Box 7000
3955 Cragwood Drive
Colorado Springs, CO 80933
1-888-775-2463
http://www.ci.org

*Compassion cares for hundreds of thousands of underprivileged children around the world through a **one-to-one sponsor program**.*

If you would like to support Compassion International around the world, please find listed below worldwide partner country mailing addresses and telephone numbers.

Compassion Australia

Box 1
Hunter Region Mail Centre
N.S.W.2310
61-2-49689999

Compassion Canada

Box 5591
London, Ontario N6A 5G8
Canada
(519) 668-0224 or (800) 563-5437

Tear Fund New Zealand

P.O. Box 8315
Auckland, New Zealand
64-9-629-1048

Tear Fund United Kingdom

100 Church Road
Teddington, Middlesex
England TW11 8QE
44-181-977-9144

SEL (Service d'Entraide et de Liaison)

9, Rue de la Gare
94234 - Cachan Cadex
France
33-1-46-65-83-03

Stichting Compassion Nederland

P.O. Box 1340
7301 BN Apeldoorn
The Netherlands
31-55-543-9750

About the Photographer

Born in 1967 to missionary parents, David Dobson grew up in India and Egypt. A high school teacher in Egypt noted David's precocious talents in photography and took him out of the classroom to be trained on location as a street photographer. By the time he graduated from high school, David's photos were already winning international awards and being shown in private exhibitions.

For the past eleven years David has traveled the world taking photos for various missions organizations. In 1995 he held an exhibition in Hollywood's famed Photo Impact Gallery that sold out on the second day. In 1997 he won the EPA award for best photo feature in a Christian publication. In addition to his world travels, David also maintains a commercial portfolio that includes directing award-winning music videos and photo assignments with international fashion accounts.

David on location in Togo.